THE LITTLE GIRL WHO DIDN'T WANT TO GO TO BED

For Alice

Credits: Amber Dusick made the dragon drawings; Myra Overby knitted the knickknacks; Maria Serfontein made the pajamas; PLAE provided Alice Bee's shoes; Samurai Scorpion appears courtesy of OWI, inc.

Special thanks to all our models: Chloe, Colman Brown, Gavin Hagerthey, Al-Tariq Elijah Harris, Nina Heppen-Ibañez, Ollie Schipani, and Josie Scripture.

ISBN 978-0-06-242537-9

The artist used software to manipulate the composite photographs for this book.
Typography by Chelsea C. Donaldson
17 18 19 20 21   SCP   10 9 8 7 6 5 4 3 2 1 • ❖ • First Edition

THE LITTLE GIRL WHO DIDN'T WANT TO GO TO BED

DAVE ENGLEDOW

HARPER

An Imprint of HarperCollinsPublishers

There once was a little girl
who didn't want to go to bed.

I DO NOT WANT TO GO TO BED

She'd rather have been
doing the laundry,

or hiding in the attic . . .

or even cleaning the toilet.

Anything would have been more fun than bedtime.

Every night, she'd make up excuse after excuse after excuse.

"I'm HUNGRY!"

"I'm NOT tired!!"

Even after the lights were out,
the little girl would lie awake
imagining all the fun that *must*
have been going on without her.

So she snuck out of her room one night, but all she saw was Mom and Dad doing boring grown-up stuff.

"Please go back to bed, dear," Mom told her.

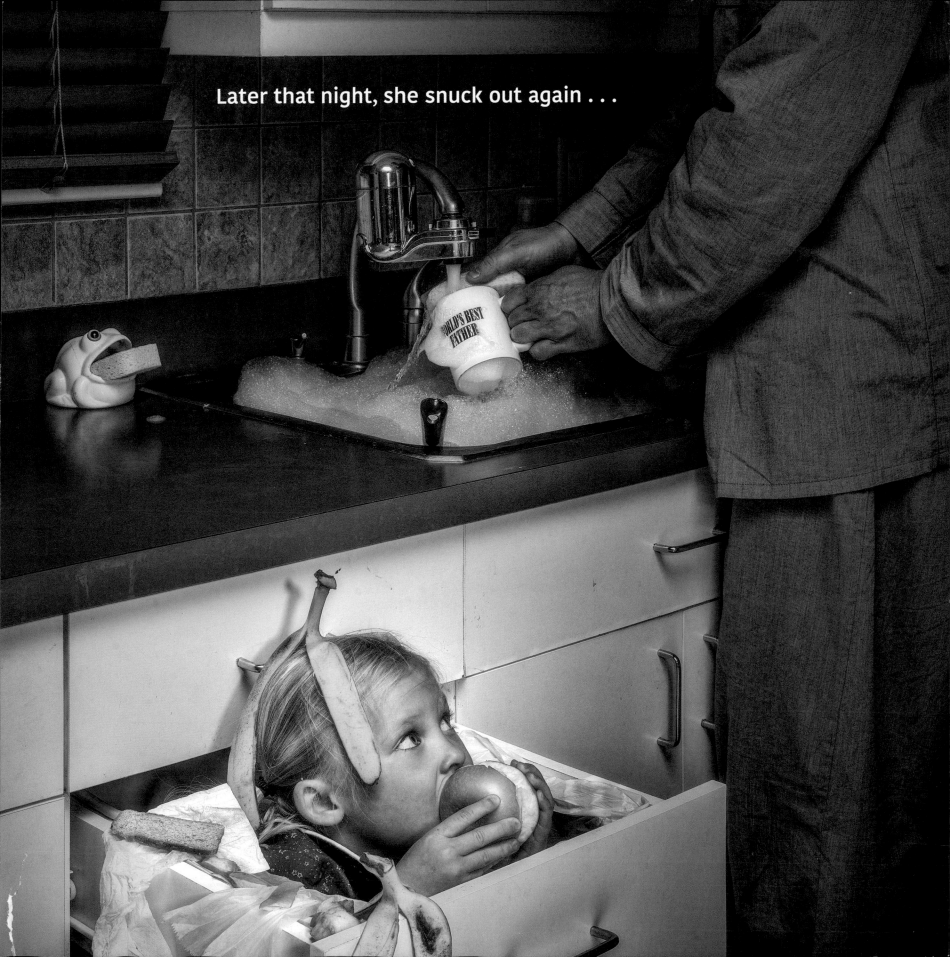

. . . but no matter where she hid, her parents sent her right back upstairs . . .

again . . .

and again . . .

and again.

Finally, Dad said to her, "If you're having trouble sleeping, why don't you try counting to yourself? Upstairs. In your room."

The little girl thought *that* was a fantastic idea.

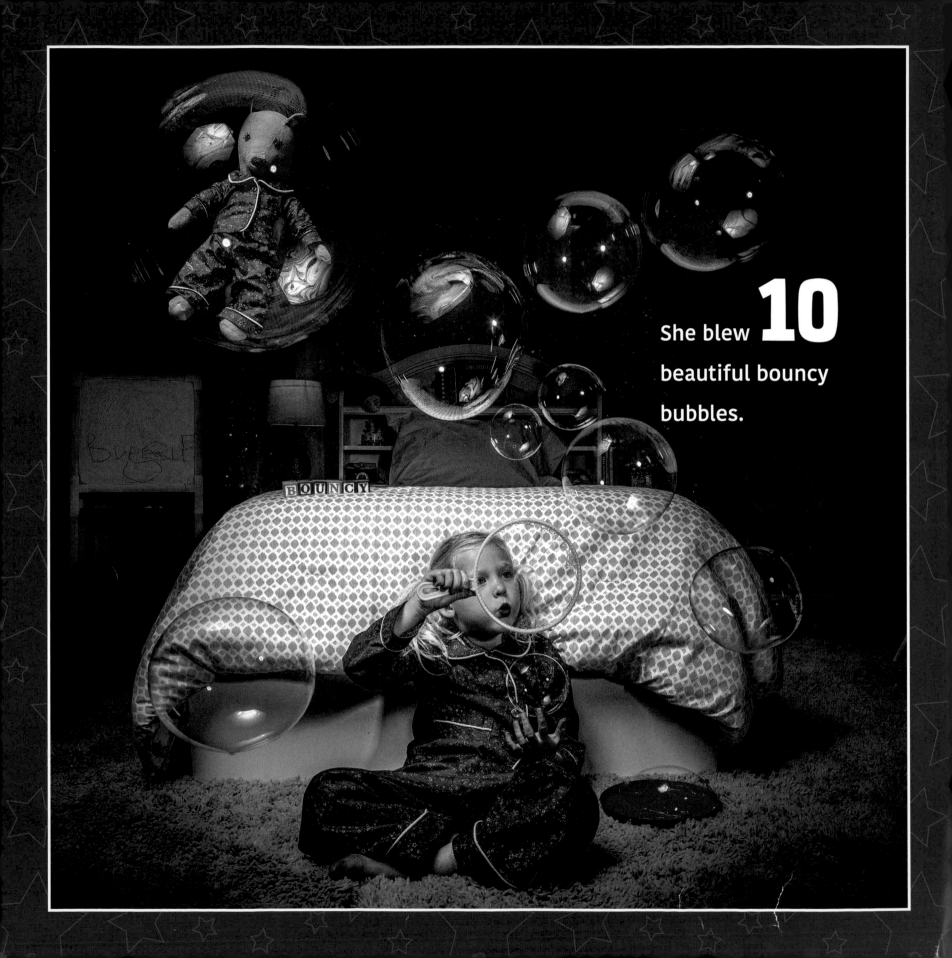

She blew **10** beautiful bouncy bubbles.

She knitted **9** knobbly knickknacks.

She sang **6** sassy sing-along songs.

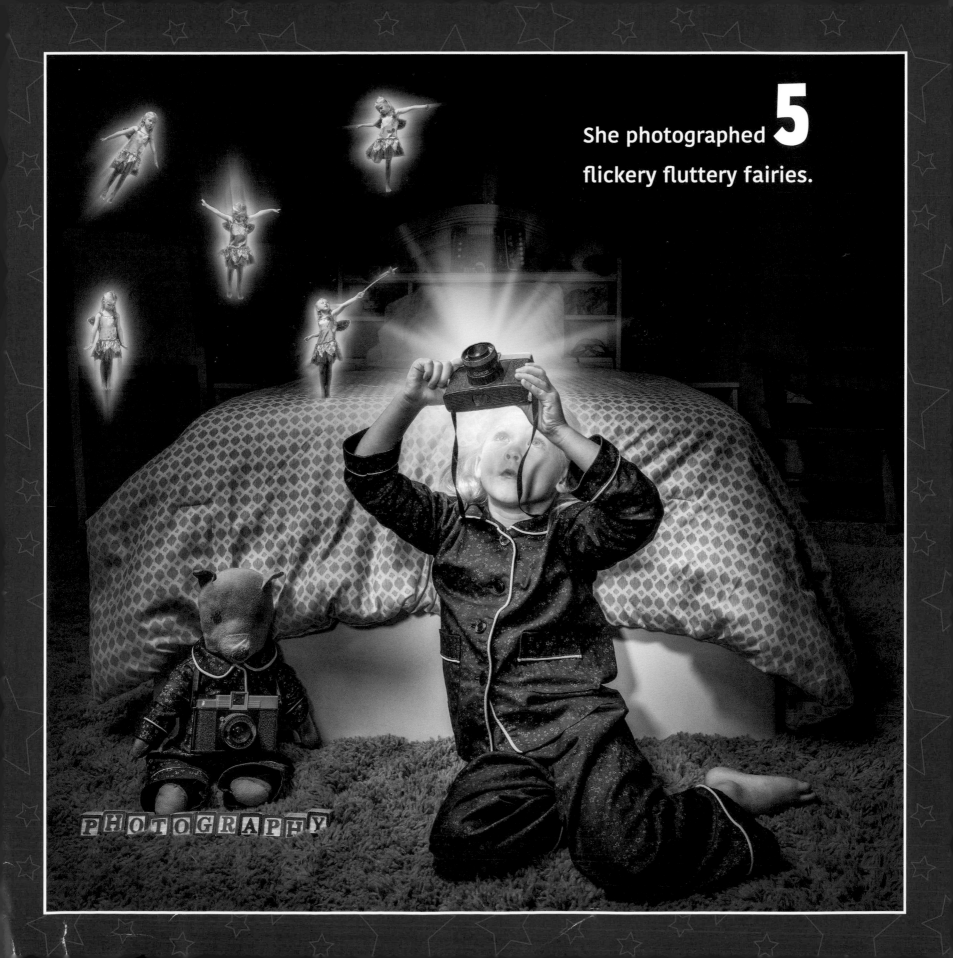

She photographed **5** flickery fluttery fairies.

She drew **4** dreamy dragon drawings.

She juggled **3** jiggly jumping jellyfish.

She sculpted **1** scary scrap-metal scorpion.

After that, she decided it was finally time to go to bed.

But just as she was getting cozy, the sun started to rise.

The little girl had stayed up *all night long*!

At breakfast, nothing went quite right for the sleepy little girl.

The peach syrup didn't pour where it was supposed to.

The milk wouldn't stay on her fork.

Her favorite straw wasn't working properly.

But at least her pancakes were soft and fluffy.

Mom sent her upstairs to get ready for the day.

"Make sure to COMB your hair and BRUSH your teeth!"

"And don't forget we have a party later.

Please wear something nice!"

Mom and Dad took her
to the park to play.

But it just wasn't as much fun as usual.

It was a beautifully
windy day . . .

which would have
been the perfect
weather . . .

to fly a kite for the
very first time . . .

if only she could have
stayed awake.

By the time the little girl arrived at the party, she was exhausted.

She missed out on all the piñata prizes . . .

. . . and didn't even get any ice cream.

During dinner, Mom and Dad couldn't stop talking about all the fun things the family had done together that day.

But the little girl couldn't remember any of it. She had slept through the best day ever.

That night the little girl fell into a peaceful sleep, dreaming about all the fun tomorrow would bring.

And Mom and Dad went back to doing their boring grown-up stuff.